BROADNECK

Happy Easter, Dear Dragon

A Follett JUST Beginning-To-Read Book

Happy Easter, Dear Dragon

Margaret Hillert

Illustrated by Carl Kock

FOLLETT PUBLISHING COMPANY

Chicago

Library of Congress Cataloging in Publication Data

Hillert, Margaret.
  Happy Easter, dear dragon.

  (Follett just beginning-to-read books)
  SUMMARY: A boy and his pet dragon celebrate Easter by enjoying the spring flowers and baby animals, coloring eggs, making an egg tree, hunting for Easter eggs, marching in the Easter parade, and going to church.
  [1. Easter stories.   2. Dragons—Fiction]   I. Kock, Carl.   II. Title.
PZ7.H558Has   [E]   79–23814
ISBN 0–695–41363–5 lib. bdg.
ISBN 0–695–31363–0 pbk.

Library of Congress Catalog Card Number: 79–23814

International Standard Book Number: 0–695–41363–5 Library binding
                                          0–695–31363–0 Paper binding

First Printing

Oh, my. Oh, my.
Come out here.
Look at this
    and this
        and this.

What pretty ones.
See here and here and here.
Red, yellow and blue ones.

7

I can make something.
Something for you.
It is pretty.
Do you like it?

8

Now come with me.
Run, run, run.
I want you to see something.

9

Look here. Look here.
Little yellow balls.
Little yellow babies.

Come look here.

Look down in here.

Little babies are here, too.

11

And see this.

One, two, three babies.

12   I like the little babies.

Oh, oh.
What is this?
See it come down.
Run, run, run.

13

Look at that.

Do you see what I see?

It is pretty.

We can make something pretty, too.

14

15

Mother, Mother.
We want to do something.
Can you guess what?
Can you help us?

17

Yes, yes.
I can guess what you want.
And I can help.

Look here.
Here is what you want.
Now get to work.
You and Father get to work.
Work, work, work.

19

Oh, my.
How pretty.
20   What good work you do.

You can do this, too.
Come and do this.
You will have to work at it.

That is good.
My! How pretty it is.
I like it.

23

Now I have something.
Something for you two.
You have to find it.
Go and look for it.

Oh, Mother.
Here it is.
And it is good to eat, too.

26

Look at us now.
We look good.
It is fun to do this.

27

I will go in here.
You can not come,
but do not go away.
I will come out.

29

30

We can go now.

Here you are with me.

And here I am with you.

Oh, what a happy Easter, dear dragon.

Margaret Hillert, author of many Follett JUST Beginning-To-Read Books, has been a first-grade teacher in Royal Oak, Michigan, since 1948.

Happy Easter, Dear Dragon uses the 68 words listed below.

a	father	like	that
am	find	little	the
and	for	look	this
are	fun		three
at		make	to
away	get	me	too
	go	mother	two
babies	good	my	
balls	guess		us
blue		not	
but	happy	now	want
	help		we
can	here	oh	what
come	how	one(s)	will
		out	with
dear	I		work
do	in	pretty	
down	is		yellow
dragon	it	red	yes
		run	you
Easter			
eat		see	
		something